The Singing Duck

by Luka Berman
illustrated by Gary R. Phillips

Once there was a little duck.
He was very happy
to be a duck.
He **liked** being a duck.

He liked his webbed feet.
They helped him swim
as fast as a fish.
He liked his sleek feathers.
They helped him stay warm
when he got wet.

He liked his duck bill.
It helped him catch bugs
and other good things to eat.

But there was one thing
the little duck didn't like.
He didn't like his quack.

"Why can't ducks sing
like other birds?"
the duck asked his mother.
"All we do is quack,
quack, quack!"

"Quack!" said his mother.
"Quack, quack, quack!"

"I want to make music,"
the duck said to himself.
"Maybe I can **learn** to sing!"

So the duck left his pond.
He waddled down a path
on his webbed feet.
He waddled under the trees.

Bird songs filled the air.

The duck saw a bluebird
in a bush.
"Tweet-tweet-tweet!"
sang the bird.
"Tweet-tweet-tweet!"

Tweet-tweet-tweet!

"Hello, bird!" said the duck.
"I like your song.
 Will you teach me to sing?"

The bluebird looked
at the duck.

"Well, thank you," she said.
"But why do you want to sing?
 You're a duck! Ducks quack."

"I don't want to quack,"
said the duck sadly.
"I want to make music.
Please teach me to sing."

The bluebird was a kind bird.
She wanted to help
the little duck.

"All right," said the bluebird.
She lifted her head.
She opened her beak wide.
She began to sing.

"Tweet-tweet-tweet!" she sang.
"Now you try it!"

The duck lifted his head.
He opened his duck bill wide.
He began to sing.

"Quack! Quack! Quack!" he sang.
"Quack, quack, quack, quack!"

Quack! Quack! Quack!

"Well," said the bird.
"I see I was wrong.
Ducks **can** sing!
I have **never** heard a duck
sing as well as you!"

That was quite true,
because the bluebird
had never heard a duck
sing at all.

"Are you sure?" asked the duck.
"Was I really singing?
 It sounded like quacking to me."

"I'm sure you were singing,"
 said the bird.
"You were happy and
 you were singing.
 Your quack **is** your song."

"Thank you, thank you!"
quacked the duck.
He waddled back to the pond
as fast as his webbed feet
could carry him.

And from then on,
the duck loved **everything**
about being a duck.